YOU WILL BE CONSUMED

BY

NIKOLAS ROBINSON

Madness Heart Press
2006 Idlewilde Run Dr.
Austin, Texas 78744

Cover by John Baltisberger

First Edition
www.madnessheart.press

To Jasmine, for being the sort of person who will actively encourage the sort of things I find entertaining and interesting to write about. Also my children, for being the motivation I needed to stick around long enough to make any of this possible...I may not still be here if it weren't for my kids.

Chapter One

As the passing train devours what feels like massive chunks of his life that he'll never be able to recapture, Michael puts his car into park and shifts his focus to the text messages he'd missed while he was driving.

He mutters angrily to himself, "Yes, DAVE, I know I'm late getting to the office this morning. Thank you soooooo much for making certain I'm aware of that."

He's so fixated on the screen of his phone that he doesn't see the homeless man approaching the car until he's forced to look up, his attention drawn by the sound of some liquid splashing onto the surface of his windshield.

Leaning into view, a disheveled and toothless man peers through the freshly moistened glass, mumbling with a smile, "Clean your windows?" The words are barely intelligible, but the context provides clarification.

Preparing to shoo the homeless man away, Michael notices the man has a partially engorged penis in one hand and a wadded up newspaper in the other. Too shocked by the sight, and admittedly-- albeit unconsciously-- jealous of the vagrant's endowment, he can't seem to think of what he was going to say.

Staring in silence, his mouth moving in a pantomime of speech, he simply watches as the strange man begins vigorously scrubbing the filthy newspaper against his windshield. His shock is reinforced as he watches the man spray additional urine onto the window before cutting off the stream and continuing to scrub at the glass surface.

The train continues rattling on by, and there are no other people around, so he remains in his car, doors securely locked, as his emotions fluctuate between anger and nervous discomfort. He momentarily considers putting the car into reverse and finding a different route to the office, preferably one with a car wash along the way. At this point, he doesn't even care that he's late for work. He would gladly accept any penalty just to get away from here.

Again, the transient passes some urine, this time onto the driver's side window; and as Michael turns to his left, his eyes meet the reddish cyclopean eye at the end of the man's urethra. It seems to almost wink at him knowingly when the man again cuts off his stream to begin scrubbing.

The windshield is filthy, as if coated in a thin layer of strawberry milk, whether due to the filthy newspaper, some manner of urinary tract infection the homeless man's experiencing, or a combination of both, Michael can't say. If the train doesn't hurry, he suspects all of his windows will be similarly obscured.

Spraying fluid and turning on his windshield wipers, Michael mitigates the worst of the mess. This elicits a frown from the homeless man, who stops where he is on the driver's side window, returns to the front, and proceeds to urinate again all over the windshield muttering, "Everyone's a critic."

With the offending penis turned away briefly, Michael risks cracking the window just slightly. He immediately wishes he hadn't because the smell of urine is overpowering, and there remains no doubt that the man is ill.

"Buddy, I will give you money if you'll please just fuck off and stop pissing on my car," he pleads.

"Gotta earn my way," the man mumbles by way of response. "Need a hamburger."

"I will buy you a dozen fucking hamburgers if you'll just god damn stop!"

The homeless man turns to look him in the eyes, and Michael reflexively puts the window back up, grateful that he'd done so only moments later as a fresh spray of urine hits the window.

"A dozen hamburgers, you say?"

Frantically, Michael nods his head, desperate to have this whole experience over with.

He rapidly removes his wallet and extracts a single $20 bill, barely cracks the window enough to slip the money through. It falls to the ground as he immediately puts the window back up.

The homeless man bends down to retrieve the cash, letting the wadded newspaper fall to the street.

The train finally completes its passage and the barriers rise. Michael breathes a sigh of relief as he shifts into drive and begins crossing the tracks.

The homeless man stands, the cash in hand, and just as Michael's rear bumper passes him by, he delicately shakes the bill and shouts, "Hey! There's piss on this!"

There's no salvaging the lost time. Michael dials the attendance line at work and leaves a brief message informing his boss that he won't be there until after lunch. If he's going to be late, it's going to be for better reasons than a train and a homeless man pissing on his car. He knows exactly where he can go to waste another couple of hours.

The club is the sort of dingy, dimly lit place that welcomed precisely the kind of audience that is in attendance. The enduring filth of the surroundings provide the perfect environment for the filth in the minds of the men as they leer at the women rhythmically gyrating on the stage.

The dancers hardly seem to notice the men or the drooling, predatory faces they present. The women who come to work in a place like this have already given up and have checked out long before they ever walk through the door. This is truly a place for the broken and the damaged, on both sides of the sordid exchange taking place. It was the perfect location for Michael to let himself forget about the transient who'd pissed all over his car before he finally rolls into work late for the day.

The current dancer, her state of undress displaying scars, stretch marks, and cellulite beneath the unforgiving fluorescents flickering above her, sweeps her vacant gaze over the crowd. In the smoky haze, she puts forth the pretense of meeting the eyes of the various men crowding the stage, but she takes in nothing, numb and focused on the music.

The audience moans inarticulately, some of them mashing clumsily through their jeans at shriveled and useless vestiges of genitals, more from habit than any sort of pleasure being derived. The dancer writhes around, tossing beads of sweat and spittle with her movements.

He allows himself to be led into the back room, where the floor is caked with decades worth of dried-up spills of liquor and various bodily fluids that hadn't been cleaned sufficiently enough. He is guided to the center of the room, just another beady-eyed patron, where he sits on a rickety wooden chair while the naked woman who brought him here dances in front of him.

She straddles his legs, leaving sticky, moist spots on the denim where she makes contact. With his left hand, he lifts a half-full beer to his lips; with his right, he massages the insignificant erection he's developing.

The way her flesh undulates before him is almost hypnotic, and the passage of time in the room becomes something irrelevant as one song bleeds into another. He forgets that he's already lost track of a significant part of his day.

She turns, bending at the waist in front of him, her ass bouncing up and down in front of his chest for a couple of minutes. She stands after a while, reaches behind her with one hand, cups the back of his neck, and pulls him down and forward until he compliantly leans toward her from his seat.

She bends at the waist again, her ass shaking inches from his face. She slowly reaches back with both hands, each one gripping a pimpled cheek and pulling them apart. With her asshole directly in front of his eyes, tiny shreds of toilet paper adhered to stray hairs are visible.

He hardly notices the way the woman's sphincter irises open, pulsing at the edges and secreting mucus that drips openly onto his lap. There's no hint of alarm or surprise in his features as, with a grinding, crunching sound of bone on bone, the already large opening wrenches wider and the dancer's hips expand unnaturally wide. She closes the distance between them steadily, her anus sliding first over his forehead and then down until it tightens around his neck, locking in place.

His hand continues caressing his erection until the signals cease transmitting from his brain to his hand.

Suffocated, he goes limp as the digestive enzymes within her anus corrode his flesh and soft tissue before finally consuming the bone.

Chapter Two

At the Trailer

Looking at her, no one would guess Anne lives the way she does. Dave understands it, though, or he thinks he does. It isn't unreasonable that she might be living in poverty. Even with the job she has, it's always less about the income itself than the debt to income ratio. Working for a collection's agency makes that sort of thing quite clear right away.He looks around the small trailer, taking in the sparse furnishings and overall poor quality of everything he's seeing. The whole place could have been outfitted with items left on curbs for trash pickup, or out of the discarded pile at a second-hand store, and he wouldn't be the least bit surprised. He's not one of those pretentious types who would make up an excuse to leave immediately upon entering the trailer, even though he's 90% certain that he'll be shaving his head to address lice after this and quite possibly coming away from the evening with numerous bedbug bites. He just finds it odd that she has been living like this without anyone knowing any better.

It finally makes sense to him that she was so hesitant to invite him over before this, and why she never invited anyone over from work, even after being there for six months. She seems nervous and a little shy as he shifts his gaze around the room, from one tattered object to another, but he isn't judging her for how she lives. He's trying to learn a little something about her from the items she's accumulated.

She isn't going to be the one to break the silence, so he decides it's up to him. "Smaller than I would have expected," he says with a warm smile and a tone that conveys no criticism.

She smiles awkwardly, something he's seen many times over the months, though he's never quite figured out what she'd been thinking. This time the smile portrays her internal struggle, unsure whether he's saying something critical or whether she can take the words at face value. He refuses to look away from her, which comes easily, and she finally accepts that he wasn't expressing judgment.

At work, she's worked her way into a position above him, despite her lack of seniority. When the old manager had stopped showing up to the office, she was a shoo-in. She always seems to know what to do, even during those rare instances when he and his other colleagues seem to be feeling lost. That self-assurance in the face of any scenario appears to be tossed out the window now that he's followed her home. He wonders if tonight is one of those occasions where he'll need to take charge and make her feel less out of her depths, but there's something in her eyes that says otherwise.

The reality is that he's not feeling any more self-assured right now than she appears to be. He had been taken aback by her, having no idea that she might be interested in him or was, as she put it, hungry for him. There'd been no indication until that night, only about an hour before they'd walked through the door of her home. The conversation had rapidly progressed from there, culminating in a kiss in the parking lot as she followed him to his car, and both of them wanted nothing more than privacy and somewhere they could continue what they'd started. It just so happened that her house was closer than his, and neither of them could think of any really good excuse to go out of the way traveling to Dave's place.

Anne's always come across as a little bit strange and maybe a little on the socially awkward side. He figures that the conversation this evening and bringing him back here is pushing the limits of her comfort zone. Admittedly, he is doing the same.

Unsure where to begin, they settle with relaxing on her beat-up and threadbare sofa, his arm around her shoulder and her head resting against him. Without cable, they watch the latter half of one inane sitcom and begin watching another before she encourages him to remove his shirt, helping him to do so. He begins feeling more relaxed, still unsure where the night might go, but accepting that this is a good sign of things to come.

The laugh track swells following something neither of them is sure was funny or even meant to be amusing, and that is when he notices that she's bitten him, taking a small piece of skin and subcutaneous fat from above his pectoral. He looks down, feeling strangely amused as she chews absently, her mouth smiling around the grinding teeth. He feels her swallow, the mechanism of her throat pressing against him as it contracts and pushes the meat down. Somewhere in the back of his mind, he questions what's just happened, but those thoughts are brushed aside along with the pain.

He tilts toward her, kissing the top of her head as she takes a second bite, using the existing cleft in his chest as ingress to get a better grip and bigger mouthful this time.

They continue watching television, though neither of them is paying much attention to the screen. The blood from his two relatively small wounds begins to mat her hair as it coagulates, but she doesn't seem to mind and, in the cramped and unclean trailer, it hardly seems that out of place.

More comfortable in his presence now, his reactions subdued, she rests her head lower. She begins chewing at the tough region just in front of his slight love handles. Her teeth slip over the flesh a few times before she succeeds in gaining some purchase, breaking the tension of collagen, and removing another mouth full of him. This most recent bite, larger than either of the previous two, makes him wince in pain for just a moment before he returns his attention to the way she's nestled up against him while a program continues on the television that he's barely been focusing on.

By the time they retire to the battered and stained mattress on the floor of her bedroom, she's taken only a couple more bites, none more substantial than the third she'd taken from his abdomen. Dave undresses quickly at her insistence, watching as she does the same. She lays back on the bed and pulls him down with her.

Their combined sweat stinging the fresh wounds, he nevertheless focuses entirely on where their bodies converge and her hunger for him takes on a wholly different nature. This, now, is the sort of thing he'd been expecting when she invited him over. He loses himself in the sensation of thrusting into her, the movement becoming more frenzied as they continue. She whimpers and moans with pleasure, and each noise escaping from her lips brings him closer to losing control.

Anne feels him tensing and preparing to pull out, and she tightens her thighs around him, her arms bracing behind his neck. She draws him deeper into her as the muscles inside of her squeeze him until the pulsing within her is milking him into her.

Dave mumbles an apology, feeling panic that he has just cum inside of her without any protection. She kisses him to shut him up. She retains her hold on him, forcing her muscles to continue throbbing around him until he's past the point of oversensitivity and has grown hard again, thrusting into her all over again.

The next time he feels himself preparing to ejaculate, he doesn't even try to separate from her as she knew he wouldn't. Together they force him even deeper as he explodes into her, truly spent this time, and beginning to feel exhausted.

He collapses onto her as gently as she knows he can, breathing heavily, his sensitive injuries burning as salt is forced into them. Still, he remains inside of her until the absence of an erection causes him to slide out. Finally, he rolls off of her and rests on his back, glazed eyes staring up at the ceiling until, without knowing it, he's fallen asleep.

Smiling her predatory smile, she drifts away to sleep herself.

He wakes to Anne biting into his thigh, her hand caressing an erection that surprises him almost as much as the new wound. No light enters through the blinds. He knows it's still night, but there is nothing in the room that tells him the time.

She bites again, and, still chewing on what she's torn away, she straddles him. At first, she simply rocks herself slightly forward and back, letting him feel the heat and the wetness of her all over him. When she's confident that she's thoroughly distracted him from the pain of his injuries she reaches down, taking his cock in her hands and guiding it back into her.

She bends forward as he is fully enveloped by her and kisses him. A tiny bit of gristle from her latest attack, still unswallowed, is passed between their mouths before she finally gulps it down. She raises herself back up so that she can take him deeper.

Impaired and almost delirious, he hardly even notices when he's ejaculated.

She remains on top of him until she's confirmed that she can't coax his weary flesh into going another time.

Lifting herself off of him, their mingled fluids dripping carelessly onto the bed and the floor, she walks naked to the kitchen, fills a glass with water, returns to the bedroom, and encourages him to drink just a little bit. He had no idea how thirsty he was until the water touches his lips, and he greedily gulps it down.

He's hardly swallowed the last drop before sleep claims him

again.

Early morning light penetrates the cracked blinds when he awakens again, this time with Anne already astride him and gyrating with a rhythm increasing steadily in tempo as she approaches orgasm. Until the moment when he erupts inside of her, he hadn't believed he still had anything left in the tank.

It isn't until shortly after she's released her hold on his now flaccid penis that he begins to feel the pain from new wounds, bites taken from all over him while he'd slept. He's momentarily astounded that he'd somehow slept through more of her feeding on him, but he feels just how tired he is. He knows that this whole experience has taken a lot out of him. For just a moment, his thoughts become clearer. Dave entertains the thought of escape, getting dressed and returning home to his comfortable bed, or maybe just checking himself in at the hospital. He knows he's too worn out to do anything of the sort. Perhaps it's just the thought of exerting the effort required to leave, or maybe it's just the admission to himself of just how weary he is that gives it power, but he falls asleep again. His mind wanders as slumber overtakes him, and he tries to remember the last time he ate anything.

The next few days pass by as a blur of fragmentary wakefulness brought on by either agony or ecstasy until he can't tell the two apart. The whole of his reality becomes her taking him into her, whether through gnashing of teeth or the sticky moistness of her vagina. There is nothing else to his existence beyond the dreamless oblivion of sleep.

Little is left of Dave when Anne finishes.

The final mouthful of his manhood fights her attempts to chew it, but perseverance wins out. He'd lost his ability to perform hours before he stopped breathing, but she waited until just before he died to begin consuming his cock, just in case, tasting herself in each bite and enjoying that flavor. He'd held out longer than she expected. Even with her narcotic influence dulling the pain and producing euphoria, shock is a real concern. In the end, blood loss and starvation competed to finish him off. She'd been betting on blood loss.

She dresses hastily, not wanting to stay in the room with the corpse any longer than necessary. On her way out, she tosses a lit match onto a pile of mail haphazardly strewn all over the dresser, and it ignites.

She sees the fire consuming the trailer in her rearview mirror as she drives slowly away in Dave's car. She feels a warm tingling between her legs that quickens her breathing. She cums one last time from the memory of what Dave has given her.

Chapter Three

"I swear to fucking Christ that there's just something about a homicide in a trailer park that almost guarantees stomachs will churn," Detective Lauren--Ren to her friends--Thomas says, shaking her head and taking in the sight of the burnt-out trailer as she steps away from her car.

Her partner, Martin Garcia, nods silently, already having gone through similar thoughts when he'd arrived on site quite a few minutes before her.

"White trash," she continues. "These people really know how to make a fucking spectacle out of killing someone."

The fire crew was still wrapping up their business when Martin had arrived, paving the way for the police to send in crime scene technicians. They'd been called in as soon as it was apparent that there was a body inside and that there were some questions surrounding the whole scenario. The fire had done a good job of damaging the body, but some rather apparent irregularities jumped out when the first officer on the scene had looked over the corpse. At least there'd been a corpse. Someone in the neighborhood had dialed 911 as soon as they'd seen smoke. If not for that, they'd probably only have a collection of ash and bone to work with. The fire department had rolled away already, leaving Martin alone with a couple of plainclothes who were setting up a perimeter and attempting to reach out to neighbors.

"Since I'm late to the party, what have I missed?"

He stares at her for a few seconds, seeing through her and not seeing her at all, something Ren's used to when he's trying to think through a problem. "I can't be sure," he begins, "but it looks like there were bites taken out of our victim before the fire started up."

"Jesus," Ren replies, shaking her head.

"His penis is gone too," he adds, almost as an afterthought.

"Excuse me?"

"Yeah," he says. "You heard me right. The ME will need to look it over, but if you ask me, based on the other apparent bite injuries, I'm pretty sure it was bitten off."

"Fucking hell," she says, unsure what else to say in response.

"Took it with 'em too, I think ... or ate it. No sign of a stray penis in the ashes," he adds. "I'm not certain, so don't quote me on this, but I'm pretty sure that sort of tissue is slow to burn."

"You know," she says, "when I said that shit about trailer trash creating a spectacle, I was talking about the fire; it wasn't meant to be a challenge."

"Don't kill the messenger," he replies. "I'm just relating what I picked up reading the scene."

She whistles lightly, shrugs her shoulders, and begins to navigate the debris, casing the scene for herself. The body had been recovered after the photos had been taken, and the scene had been marked off. Sifting through the wet ash with a pen, she has to acknowledge that it's going to take a while before the place can be adequately inventoried.

Pulling up the photos her partner had taken the liberty of snapping with his cell phone and sent to her, she reorients herself to match the angles and zooms in on the places he'd noted as being likely bite wounds, including the blackened stub just above the shriveled and hardly recognizable testicles. Pulling up various shots he'd taken, she has to concede that it does seem like the man had been chewed up pretty badly and that the penis more than likely went the same way.

"Seriously," she mutters, "What the fuck?"

"My thoughts exactly," Martin replies from immediately behind her. She almost jumps but catches herself. She'd been so caught up in analyzing the things he'd documented while the body was still there that she hadn't heard him coming up behind her.

"Creepy asshole," she laughs. "How many times do I have to tell you not to sneak up on me like that?"

"I'll give you the same answer I always do," he grins. "At least that one time."

The place is thoroughly gutted. Fire always eats right through a trailer and between the flames and the high-pressure water jets from the hoses the fire department deployed, the place is wrecked.

"Neighbors see anything?" she asks him without looking away from the charred remains of a mattress.

"No clue," he shrugs. "None of them will answer their doors for cops. You know how it is."

"A.C.A.B." Ren and Martin are both intimately familiar with the slogan, All Cops Are Bastards. It's impossible to avoid it in their profession.

"You've got it."

"Fucking meth head trailer trash," she says, shaking her head slightly and frowning at the surrounding homes.

"Not this one, though," he says. "No sign of this being a lab mishap or any sort of explosion."

She grumbles in affirmation, still looking around at the other trailers nearby.

"Dollars to donuts," he says after a pause, "this victim was dead before the trailer went up."

"Trying to cover up the murder, you think?"

He shrugs and gives her a crooked smile. "I haven't got a fucking clue, being honest. This whole thing is a shit show, and we'll be lucky if we have anything to go on when it's all said and done."

"So, I suspect you're thinking those are human bite marks?"

"No dead animals in the rubble, and they sure as shit looked human to me. I'd be lying if I tried to pretend that isn't exactly where my mind has gone with it."

She doesn't reply, but based on the details she can make out from his pictures, they don't look like animal bites to her either.

The two of them continue sifting through the mess and the final officer leaves after cordoning off the area with yellow tape.

Alone and finding no answers in the former residence, they both become acutely aware that they're losing daylight. Under the circumstances, neither of them are comfortable sticking around the disreputable neighborhood after dark.

As the same words almost leave her mouth, Martin says, "What the fuck are we dealing with here?"

"Your guess is as good as mine," she replies.

"Lot manager says this place was abandoned for more than a month ago, when I reached him over the phone. But he says he doesn't come down this way if he can avoid it. Sounds like a slumlord asshole to me. Could have been someone squatting here, though."

She looks from him to the nearest trailer, catching the curtain rustling as she does so. "Well, I guess we have to check with the neighborhood watch," she says, gesturing to the place next door.

Stepping gingerly through the gap where a wall used to be, they cross the intervening space to the home next door. He climbs the rotting wooden stairs ahead of her and raps heavily at the door. "Police! Open up! We have some questions about what happened here today!"

His voice carries through the surrounding lot, more than likely drawing unwanted attention. The sounds of furtive movements and hissed whispers carry through the door and poorly insulated walls of the mobile home, but there is no response to his knock.

"Be careful," Ren whispers harshly. They've both witnessed how unstable junkies can be. This whole neighborhood has traditionally consisted of nothing but the lowest of human vermin, sex offenders and drug addicts congregating in their perverse little haven.

He knocks again after a minute. "We know you're home! We just want to ask you some questions!"

Still, no one answers and they both wonder if this is the time when someone starts recklessly shooting through the door. The noise is surely attracting the attention of the other neighbors, who are more than likely equally enthusiastic about cops parading around. Both of them know that things could get ugly and that any one of the residents of this park could be the killer they believe they're looking for.

"Fuck this," Martin mutters and Ren has only a split second to regret letting him be the point man when approaching the door. Fragmentary flashes of his previous lapses in impulse control streak through her mind in the time it takes for him to brace himself against the unsteady rail of the porch. He kicks the door open with a loud crack that echoes through the trees and the rest of the trailer court.

In the gloomy, poorly lit living room now exposed to the outside, two tweakers huddle together in shock and fear. Greasy and pimpled, dotted with scabs, neither the boy nor the girl can be older than their mid-20s, though their lifestyle has taken a hefty toll on them.

Martin walks through the open door, glancing around and seeing no one but the two degenerates in front of him. "Anyone else here?" he asks politely as if he hadn't just broken into their home.

Both of the frightened kids shake their heads, cowering away from the two detectives standing in the room and looming over them.

"What's this you have here?" Martin asks as he points to the cluster of nearly transparent crystals piled up at the center of the coffee table. "It looks like you've got more money invested in that shit right there than in this beat-up hovel you're living in. Did you two rob your dealer or something?"

She glances over at the methamphetamine and paraphernalia collected on the table and has to agree with his assessment. These two are in possession of easily $10,000 worth of what appears to be high-quality crystal meth.

"We're not here for the drugs," Ren says, trying to sound calm and reassuring. "Something awful happened just next door, and we're hoping you saw something."

She must have measured her tone appropriately, because it doesn't take more than a few seconds before the two of them are jabbering over one another, rambling like a couple of agitated chimps. She and Martin are hard-pressed to keep up with the two addicts, and they have to interject occasionally just to get one or the other to repeat something that didn't make any sense. Most of the time, it still didn't make any sense.

The two babbling junkies claim some pretty lady started squatting in the empty trailer a month back, or a few weeks before, time doesn't seem to mean much to them. She kept to herself, for the most part, they say, but she had come back with a guy maybe four days before, and she took off just before the fire got going. Neither of the tweakers had seen the guy leave, but they weren't certain he hadn't been in the car with the lady when she took off in such a hurry.

No license number, only a vague description of the car and an even more uselessly vague description of the woman who was more than likely their suspect: they don't have much more to go on than they had before he'd kicked the door in.

She thanks them anyhow and apologizes for the damage to the door. The two kids are too grateful for not being in trouble to care about that, though.

Ren prepares to leave when she catches the look on Martin's face. They've worked together for a long time, and she's familiar with all of his expressions, or she thinks she is.

"Are you fucking pouting about something?" she asks, genuinely perplexed by the goofy, puppy dog contortion of his features.

Grinning, he glances pointedly at the drugs on the coffee table without moving anything but his eyes. "What you said about us not being here for the drugs. How firm were you in that stance?"

"What?"

"Well," he replies, "maybe we could get high a little bit, you know, before we take off."

Ren stares at him, jaw wide and head tilted. She attempts to speak multiple times, but no words come out because she can't think of where to begin.

He gestures to the junkies, "They won't mind." The two still sitting together on the floor where they'd initially cowered begin nodding vigorously after a delay of no more than 15 seconds processing what he'd said.

Chapter Four

Their minds still spinning like errant pinwheels, the two detectives try to contain their excess energy while they wait for the Medical Examiner, Stephen Lee, to finish his preliminary exam. She, for the most part, manages to maintain her composure, while he paces back and forth, chewing on his lip while his shoes squeak out an irritating rhythm on the tile.

Minutes seem to dilate just like their pupils, but the ME finally sighs, removes his gloves, and acknowledges their presence.

"There are tests that need to be run before I can give you any conclusive details about some major irregularities," Stephen begins. "But I do have some answers that may only produce additional questions. Those questions, I may not be able to answer for a while, if at all."

"We'll take what we can get," she replies.

"Shit," Martin interjects. "We will take anything at all right now."

"Well, from a superficial analysis of the numerous wounds, I can say for sure they were inflicted over a period of days, maybe even weeks, rather than all at once." He looks back and forth between them before addressing the unasked question, "Definitely human bite marks."

"So, you're telling us that someone was snacking on this guy, one bite at a time?" She stares at Stephen, uncertain whether this is some sort of gallows humor.

The ME goes on, his expression betraying no indication he was joking, "That does seem to be the truth of it. More bizarre is the fact that there are no signs of ligature marks or restraint of any kind. I'll have to wait for a full blood panel, but if this guy was restrained, it was entirely chemically."

"How long until we know what they used to drug him?" Martin asks.

"This is a rush order, but it's still going to take a day or two to get anything back from the lab."

"Shit"

"Hopefully they don't screw anything up at the lab," Stephen adds. "There wasn't much blood to work with in the first place. In fact, if you put me on the spot, I'm guessing blood loss or trauma for the cause of death, but I'll be a while determining which wound put the nail in this poor bastard's coffin."

"So," she begins, glancing at Martin while he chews on his lower lip and taps his foot nervously, "my partner here is just dying to hear about the penis." She smiles as she finishes.

"Fucking thank you!" he replies, with a grin. "What about the penis, doc?"

"The penis was severed post-mortem, and like the other injuries, it does appear to have been removed with human teeth as the offending instrument as well."

Martin winces as his suspicion is confirmed. "At least he was already dead when that happened. But still, what the fuck?"

"What the fuck, is right," Ren says, feeling soberer by the minute and wishing this whole conversation could be written off as some meth-fueled psychological break.

"Indeed," the ME replies. "A cursory examination leads me to believe that most of the lacerations were made while our John Doe here was alive; but there are a few, like the penis, that I'm certain are post-mortem as well."

"So, assuming those tweaks weren't shining us on," Martin begins, "we have a young woman, squatting in this trailer, who brings a man back with her somewhere between a few days and a week ago. She spends those days drugging the guy and taking bites out of him until he bleeds to death, and then she continues eating him before finally torching the place on her way out?"

"Unfortunately," Stephen replies, "that does appear to be an accurate statement of the facts as we presently understand them."

"You left out the part where she bit off his cock on the way out the door," she adds with a smirk as she glances at Martin.

He grimaces in response. "I really don't know how I feel about that. On the one hand, at least maybe he was dead before she chomped it off." He pauses, motioning with his hands like a scale set out of balance. "On the other hand, she did potentially bite the dick off a cadaver. That is just objectively unsettling."

The ME chuckles nervously as he replies, "I have to admit that I'm with you on that one."

Encouraged, Martin says, "Personally, I'm not sure why she didn't cook the meat before eating it."

With nothing further to learn so early in the examination, they excuse themselves and leave the morgue. They're both hoping that the tox screen and full autopsy might provide them with some sort of explanation that makes sense of the bullshit that's been tossed in their laps.

Chapter Five

A couple of days pass before Ren and Martin are called to investigate another strange body found at the landfill.

They arrive at the same time, but she takes her time getting out of the car just the same.

"Let me tell you," Ren says as she finally opens the door, "there is no place I'd rather be than the fucking landfill."

Martin shrugs in response and says nothing, barely succeeding in suppressing the grin that threatens to spoil his apparent commiseration. He always actually sort of liked junkyards, landfills, and places like this.

Even though he doesn't mind the dump, he has to admit it is an awful place to be on a hot day, flies buzzing all around along with the never-ending squawking of the seagulls making for an unpleasant experience.

They both hate the fucking place right now, but when a body shows up in a pile of trash, there's no way for them to avoid being present.

"Do you bring all the girls here?" she asks as she carefully makes her way to where he's standing.

"Only the truly special ones," he says with a wink. He barely manages to stifle a chuckle before whispering, "Now fuck off with that shit," hoping that the other officers won't overhear the conversation.

They are quick to make their way up the man-made hill of refuse to where the yellow tape cordons off a sizable chunk of undesirable real estate. Two patrol officers wait for them, grim expressions on their faces. The officer immediately to her left, she notes as they approach, appears to have just vomited or come close, based on his pallor and the look on his face.

They step past the boundary of the crime scene and see one of the technicians already kneeling near the body. It takes Martin only a moment to pick up on what likely led to the officer losing his lunch.

"Where's the fucking head?"

The technician from the coroner's office glances up, only now noticing he's not alone with the body any longer. "It's not here," the young man answers.

"Well, that certainly helps," he replies.

"Shut up," she hisses, hoping her partner's sarcasm won't be an issue.

"Fine," he whispers back with an exaggerated pout on his face. "But we still don't know about the missing head."

"I doubt we're going to find it anywhere nearby," the technician says, rising to his feet. "We can't know for sure without tests, but that damage around the neck, and even some on the upper vertebrae there," he points to the neck, "looks like it was in contact with something corrosive, maybe an acid of some kind."

"Wait," Martin replies. "Someone poured acid over this guy's head until it was dissolved? That's some seriously cruel shit."

"More likely, he was dipped into the acid upside down and kept there," the technician says. "There's no evidence of it spilling or splashing onto his shoulders or chest like we'd see if it was dumped over his head. Besides, acids and corrosives don't act as fast in real life as they do in the movies."

"That doesn't make it sound any better," she says, lowering herself to her haunches to get a better look at the body where the head should connect. "How long would it take, hanging someone in a vat or barrel of acid, to remove the head like this?"

"Depending on the acid, it could be hours or even days to get that kind of result," he replies. "If it was something particularly corrosive, it could be minutes, I guess."

"Good lord," Martin says, "that really doesn't narrow it down too much."

"Nope," the technician says casually as he loads his samples into their specific places in his case. "We'll have that sort of detail within the next couple of days."

"Thanks," she says absently from where she's still staring at the stump only slightly protruding above the man's shoulders.

Her partner begins processing the scene his own way, nudging debris aside with the toes of his shoes, looking for nothing in particular but hoping he'll know what he's looking for when he sees it.

She's the one who notices the first useful detail, happening to glance at the victim's hand. "There's some sort of symbol here," she says. Attempting to only minimally disturb the body, Ren shifts the arm just enough that she can better see the marking on the dead man's hand.

"Strip club," he says, leaning down behind her to get a better look for himself.

"Degenerate," she mutters as she looks back at him with a grin.

"Gives us a place to start, I suppose. A lot of this trash is from the same place. Vegas odds put this guy in the dumpster out back of that place before he wound up catching a ride here."

"You sound pretty proud of yourself," she says as she gets to her feet.

"Found us a valuable lead, didn't I?"

"Because you're a filthy pervert who hangs out in dives where women take their clothes off for money," she replies, barely able to keep herself from laughing as she struggles to maintain a matronly tone. "Also, need I remind you that I found the stamp on his hand?"

"You use the word dive, but I don't think you know what that word means yet." He winks. "You'll know soon, though. Shall we be off?"

The drones and pulses of the music can be heard where they park their cars on the street outside of the club. The worn brick facade appears not to have been maintained since the building was constructed sometime in the previous century. The windows are blacked out and littered with faded advertisements for alcohol and cigarette brands.

"You've got to be fucking kidding me," she mutters, the disdain in her voice only halfway in jest. "You actually spent time at this place? Willingly?"

"You ain't seen anything yet," he replies as a smirk plasters itself over his face. "Just wait until we get inside."

"Do we have to?"

"It'll be a treat, I assure you."

With a flourish, he opens the door for her and, as they enter, their eyes have to adjust to the sudden darkness of the interior. The first thing she notices is that there aren't any stages or dance floors immediately visible upon walking through the door. In front of them is a bar with a scantily clad girl behind it, prepared to take their orders or change out larger bills for something more accommodating to the environment.

The music feels like it is coming from all directions now that they're inside, but it's easy for her to see where the entrance to the stages is located.

"This is about as far as I ever made it in here," he shouts to be heard over the throbbing bass. "I dated a bartender who worked here when I was in college."

They make their way over to the bar where the girl--or woman, Ren can see she's older than she initially appeared now that the heavy makeup can be more clearly seen--waits expectantly. The bartender appears to be preparing to speak as she flashes her badge, and there is a momentary flicker of discomfort and disappointment before the bartender composes herself.

She reaches out of sight slowly, to avoid appearing as a threat, and turns down the music. "There's no one dancing, is what I wanted to tell you, and there's no one else here right now. The music is just for me."

"Is it usually just you here at this time of day?"

"More often lately," she replies with a shrug. "A lot of the girls have been flaking out and not coming in, and I can't say I'm altogether too hurt by that. No girls means no perverts, so it's mostly just been me in here the last few days."

The detectives look at one another, both of them thinking something is off about the situation. He's the first to bring attention to one of the things that feels off about the place. "Isn't there supposed to be security of some kind, a bouncer or something?"

"He hasn't been in the last couple of days, either, and the owner doesn't seem too concerned about it. He's already not thrilled to be paying for me to be here when there are no customers."

"Mind if we look around a bit?"

"Knock yourselves out," she replies dismissively. "Okay if I turn the music back up a bit?"

"I don't care," Ren says, looking at Martin as he shrugs. Before they've turned to begin looking over the place, the music is back up about halfway to where it was when they arrived.

The place is as empty as the bartender indicated. No sign that there had been a single customer all day. The floors, tables, and stages are as close to spotless as they could be in an establishment like this.

"Kind of a shithole," she comments as they work their way to the curtained doorway at the rear of the main floor.

"I told you so," he replies.

The private rooms and dressing room are as empty and relatively clean as the rest of the establishment, and though they didn't know what they would be looking for when they arrived, they know they haven't found it yet.

"We'll have to come back once we have an ID for the victim," he says, as they return through the main dance floor after exploring the rest of the area backstage. "Maybe the bartender will have some information for us once we have a photo for the dead guy. Hopefully, some of the girls will actually be here too at that point."

"I wouldn't hold my breath on that," she says.

They return to the bar. "Thanks for your time," she says to the bartender as they prepare to leave.

"No problem," she replies as she pours herself a drink.

As they cross the threshold back to the outside world, Ren turns back to the bartender. "Stay safe and be careful, okay?" She doesn't know where the impulse comes from, but she trusts her instincts.

The bartender smiles warmly in response. "Always."

The door closes and the interior of the club is shut away again as if it belongs to a different world, though the music has been turned back up because it's just as loud as it had been when they arrived.

Chapter Six

"What the fuck does he mean, negative?" Ren can't believe what her partner's relaying.

"I asked the ME that same question when he told me the news."

"How can the toxicology report be negative? What did this bitch use to drug our victim?"

He ponders his response for a moment. "Well, if the lab is to be believed, and our ME assures me they tested for everything under the sun, he wasn't drugged by anything they tested for. Our boy, Dave, was stone-cold sober while he was providing the main course."

"That doesn't make a god damn bit of sense," Ren replies, exasperated. The wheels are turning in her mind as she tries to make sense of the insane. "Was he hypnotized or something?"

"You know what, I don't believe in any of that shit, and there's no way to test for it anyhow," he says. "But I'd rather believe that than accept that this seemingly normal guy offered himself up as some sort of fucked up sacrifice. So, hypnosis and cult brainwashing are both definitely on the table at this point."

They stand together in silence, not sure where to go from here. The fire had destroyed anything they might have been able to use for identification. They'd had a hard enough time identifying the victim after the state he was in from the fire. It was too much to hope that the scattered, nonsense-riddled, and vague description provided by the neighbors might produce a viable lead of any kind.

"This trail is going cold, isn't it?" she asks, wishing either of them would think of something they might have overlooked.

"Fucking frigid," he confirms, resigning himself to the fact that this one is destined for the mocking pile of unsolved homicides that have been building up.

"Truth is," he adds after a pause, "we were never going to catch this one. These fucking weird ones lately are stacking up in a way I really don't like."

"I've been feeling the same," she replies. "What the fuck is going on around here?"

He grins, but the amusement doesn't fully extend to his eyes. The eyes betray uncertainty and fear that he's trying hard to mask behind a facade. "I'm thinking aliens maybe, or it could be that someone opened a portal to Hell, you know, or something close enough to be indistinguishable. And now all sorts of awful shit is slipping out and making a mess in our world. Hell, it could be that we're dead, or one of us is, and this is just some fucked up fever dream one of us is experiencing as the lights go out."

He glances over at her and seeing no reaction to his attempt at humor, he continues. "Honestly, I wouldn't be the least bit surprised if any of those things happen to be true at this point."

She finally does smile. "Fuck me if I can think of a better explanation."

"You're on," he replies with a smirk. "If you can come up with a more sensible explanation for all of this shit lately, you deserve it."

And even though she doesn't think of a better explanation, they still end up at his place that night. He'd set aside some of the crystal appropriated from the junkies for just such an occasion; hoping that an all-night, amphetamine-fuelled fuck fest might just succeed in taking their minds off the seemingly never-ending cascade of failure to close these weird cases.

As their hearts race and the bedding becomes soaked in sweat and the other fluids they're releasing, they do manage to forget for just a little while. For at least those few hours, the rest of the bullshit they're dealing with doesn't exist.

Chapter Seven

The high begins wearing off, and both of them are ready to sleep. Ren prepares to leave, cleaning herself up from the evening's activities.

"We already shit where we eat, so there's really no harm in taking it a step further," Martin insists from the bed, on his side, propped up by his left arm.

"I am not moving in with you," she replies to the question he didn't ask.

His face contorts like a sullen child, pouting exaggeratedly. They've had this conversation multiple times in the past, and it always comes down to the same argument from her perspective. "Hey, you've got plenty of your own baggage, too. It wouldn't be so bad."

"Yes, we all have baggage," she says patiently. "The difference is that you insist that yours is carry-on while the rest of us stow ours in the belly of the plane, out of sight, if you follow me."

"You think you're funny, don't you?"

She offers a toothy grin in response.

"Fine," he says, cracking a smile of his own. "I admit that was pretty witty, but you're still an asshole."

"And," she adds, "I am still going home."

"Drive the dagger right in, why don't you?" He falls back on the mattress, dramatically clutching his chest and grimacing.

She finishes dressing while he rolls back and forth across the mattress in an absurd, melodramatic pantomime of an excruciating death. As she walks to the door, she doesn't even look back his way before saying, "I'll see you in the morning. Don't be so dramatic."

Martin's spent many nights with Ren, caressing her with his adoring hands until he finally started falling asleep, loving the feel of her skin. The texture, so smooth and lovely. For years now, since they became lovers in addition to being partners, he's admired the way she felt under his hands and pressed closer to the rest of him.

Now that he lays alone in his bed, staring wakefully at the ceiling with her skin draped over his own, it doesn't feel quite the same. He wishes he could take it all back, that he'd never peeled it away to keep it for himself.

He remembers how she struggled.

He recalls, quite clearly, the look of hurt and betrayal in her brown eyes, so excruciating to him even as he continued flaying her. It seems so much worse now, knowing it was all for nothing.

He can't even recall now why he'd decided he needed her skin for himself, even though it had seemed so important at the moment. The motivations remain mysterious in retrospect. There hadn't been any fighting. Ren hadn't threatened to leave him, and he had no cause to suspect she was thinking about it. All he can remember clearly was that he felt an overwhelming need to have her flesh for himself.

Fragmentary daydreams and fantasies come back to him, fleeting things that had flowed through his mind as he'd gone to work on skinning her. Prancing around his house, nude, with only her hide draped over him like a robe. He saw himself rolling back and forth on the bed, her flesh soothing his own like satin sheets. In his mind, he'd envisioned himself sliding her skin against himself after shaving his body hairless in a hot bath.

None of these things, he knows now, would have been practical. He had wasted his time, and he had wasted her death, and now he would never be able to feel her again.

He begins crying, and his eyes are moist when he wakes up from the terrible nightmare. He frantically searches for Ren beside him, and it takes a minute before he remembers that she left for the night and is staying at her own house. If she'd been there, she'd have surely tried to wake him. It's obvious he's been thrashing around.

It's been years since he's experienced night terrors, and he's stunned by the residual effects of the dream as he attempts to shake the sensations that still feel so real to him. He actively fights the urge to call Ren at 3 AM to make sure she's ok, knowing she will be bitter about it for days.

He knows that he needs to will himself through this panic. The nightmares began when he was a child, even before he'd become aware he was growing up with a father whose temper was often volatile, and who often exploded with fits of violence and terror for both his mother and himself. The actual night terrors, as he came to know them, didn't start until his mother's death at his father's hands. His father's suicide immediately following probably didn't help, either, nor did the subsequent half an hour he spent alone in a house with the dead bodies of his parents before the police arrived following a concerned neighbor's call reporting the gunfire.

The officers who arrived and took him outside had been the first people to show him any real compassion during those formative years of his life, and that memory stuck with him through foster care with an aunt and uncle he'd never met until he was going to live with them. The recollection of the cops' kindness influenced his decision to become one himself, even if he wasn't always conscious of this being the case.

His daily life has been filled with horrors that sometimes put his own earliest memories to shame, and yet the nightmares had stayed away until now.

There won't be any sleep for the rest of the night.

He gets out of bed and wanders into the living room. He flops back on the sofa, flips through some channels for adequate background noise, taps out a line of cocaine from his hidden stash, and remotely connects his laptop to the office network.

Settled there in his living room, he begins to browse through cases over the previous few months. He's looking for anything involving homicides that seem unusual, and he flags a few for further evaluation. There are hours left before he has to head in for work, and he wants to at least try to sort some things out before he meets up with Ren in the morning.

Chapter Eight

It had been a relatively chilly couple of nights to be working the streets, and she'd struck out the night before. She could suck it up and capitalize on the fact that plenty of the other girls had given up and returned to whatever passed for home, opting to be warm and comfortable instead of making money. It was a simple calculation on her part to consider it worthwhile, to venture out in the miserable weather.

Here she was, putting that college education to good use again, standing in the drizzling rain, waiting for some desperate man to come along, flashing money and hoping she'd join him for an hour or two. Surely someone would show up and get her out of the cold.

Hours passed, as did several vehicles, and she was reconsidering the benefits of being out on the sidewalk when the pristine BMW slows as it approaches her. Her heart races just slightly, knowing that this could potentially be her meal ticket.

The professionally groomed man behind the steering wheel

smiles at her as she leans down to look through the lowering passenger-side window, and she smiles back.

"What are you looking for tonight, handsome?" she asks.

"I'd say I was looking for you," he replies.

"It's fifty dollars upfront and another fifty per hour," she says.

He reaches into the inside pocket of his jacket and extracts a wallet, slipping a single fifty dollar from within and extends his arm across the empty passenger seat to hand it to her.

She accepts the crisp bill and climbs into the open passenger-side door of the sedan. The John behind the wheel looks like he'll be an easy mark, and she expects to walk away with a shit load more than $50 for the night's work.

The following morning, her body rests, exsanguinated and bruised, beneath a pile of garbage.

Chapter Nine

The ID on the dead man from the landfill doesn't ring any bells with the bartender from the strip club, and again there are no dancers present when they return with the photo and the name.

There is one significant lead that pops up as they dig into the information about the victim; he was employed by the same company as the arson victim from the trailer park. It's a small insurance company in a squat, nondescript building; the sort of place she's always thought of as a cubicle farm.

The dead man had been missing since before the first one they'd discovered by a couple of days. In addition to the two dead men, there was another man and a woman who hadn't come into work for nearly the same length of time.

They collect the additional names and contact information from a concerned Human Resources representative, confident that they are finally on the right track. That brief surge of confidence dissipates rapidly when each address turns out to be a non-starter.

"Well, fuck." Martin drops heavily into the passenger seat and pulls the door closed forcefully.

"My thoughts exactly," Ren says. "It's starting to feel like there's some capricious god playing games with us at this point."

"Did you just say capricious?"

She raises the middle finger of her right hand without looking at him before she starts the car and pulls away from the curb.

"What? I thought it was cute."

Ignoring him, she asks, "Are you hungry?"

"I could eat."

"Good," she replies. "This is a perfect opportunity for some stress eating."

"Back to square zero after all," he agrees.

They take their time over lunch, mulling over the cases silently and desperately struggling to put the pieces together into some sort of coherent picture. Neither of them is having any luck, but they're both too stubborn to give up, too proud, and at this point, too invested.

He startles her when he finally speaks, derailing her train of thought. "I wonder if that bartender has contact info for the absentee dancers?"

"Excuse me?"

"Sorry. I was sort of thinking out loud," he says. "But, it might be worth checking to see if the girls are legitimately missing too, like these other four appear to be."

"And here I thought you were just trying to get some private dances."

"Only from you, baby," he says with a smile.

The bartender doesn't appear to be any happier to see them when they walk through the door for the third time than she had during either of the previous visits, even though, by the look of things, they were the only people walking through the door.

When they leave, it's with addresses and phone numbers for five dancers and the absent bouncer.

No one answers the phone at any of the phone numbers when

he calls them while she drives to the bouncer's address. He leaves voicemails, but he has a sinking feeling that there won't be any return phone calls. He has no particular reason to feel the way he does, but the whole situation is starting to get under his skin.

Ren feels the same way, but she masks it better. To be a woman in a male-dominated profession like hers, she learned a long time ago to suppress her outward emotional responses better than the men around her.

Over the subsequent hour, they knock on four doors with no answer and no sign that anyone has been home. Mail sits, collecting in a mailbox at one house, and newspapers accumulate in the sheltered porch of another.

Neither of them can fully suppress the growing tension with each failed step toward a resolution that keeps evading them. At their fifth stop, a red-headed girl answers the door who's pretty for her age. She confirms that she had been a dancer at the club until she found a better offer somewhere that charged her less for stage rent. It helped that it was somewhere she didn't have the constant suspicion that she would be raped at any time.

She states aggressively that she hasn't been in contact with any of the girls from her former place of employment, nor anyone else.

He attempts to thank her for her time, but she spends a little while longer venting about how the clients and the other girls there had started to seem creepy to her. "The whole environment," she says, "just started feeling weird to me."

"Weird?" Ren interrupts. "Would you mind clarifying what you mean by that?"

"Just, even the girls started to look different, like they weren't taking care of themselves and weren't all there anymore, you know, like in the head. I caught people looking at me in a funny way, too, sometimes, like hungry, but not the good way, like when I'm happy on stage. Some of the other girls too, they looked at me weird like that. Made my skin crawl."

"Thanks," Ren replies as she hands the girl both of their business cards. "If we have any other questions, we might call you. If you think of anything else, please call either of us."

"That last little bit didn't make me feel any better about what's going on right now," he mutters as they drive toward the final address on their list.

"You're telling me," Ren replies. "That girl almost had me shivering."

"Yeah, I've had a skin-crawling sensation most of the day, and her description of working conditions was unsettling."

"I bet that's why the bartender hasn't been too broken up about no one showing up lately. Her lack of concern was a touch disconcerting at first, but now I think I might understand," she says.

"I'd feel a bit more casual about being there alone if the alternative was always being on the edge and creeped out," he agrees.

The final stop greets them with an open door and unwelcoming darkness beyond the threshold. Neither of them are eager to do what they know they have to do. But training kicks in, and they fall back on letting it lead the way.

She hasn't made it up the front steps to the wooden porch before a peculiar and unpleasant odor reaches her nose. A glance to the left tells her that he also picked up on it.

"What the fuck is that?" he whispers, just loud enough for her to hear.

"No idea."

They both ensure their firearms are prepared to be drawn as they cross the porch, and she takes the lead, knocking at the frame of the open door.

"Ashley, this is the police," she says, her voice projecting authority and confidence she doesn't feel. "We have some questions for you."

Silence is the only response, and she repeats herself louder.

"I'm calling it in," he says when the second attempt to get attention meets with no result. He notifies dispatch of their location and the circumstances, advising that they are going inside.

With additional units en route, they step through the door. Ren feels around for the light switch and the dark is transformed into a brightly lit living room. She calls out again for Ashley, and again there is nothing but silence in return.

Without a word, they spread out to investigate their immediate surroundings. The room isn't clean, but there's none of the disarray associated with a struggle taking place. The silence feels like an unwanted third occupant of the room, poised as if ready to devour them at any moment for daring to disturb it.

"There's a weird stain on the sofa over here," he says. "Not just the sofa, actually." As he's speaking, he kneels to get closer, to examine the fluid. "That smells fucking terrible," he says. "I think we found the source of that god awful odor."

She approaches the sofa for a better look, seeing the other puddles he'd hinted at as well. It appears brownish, just that side of red, with a viscous, oily quality to it, and bits of matter are suspended in it.

"Smell this," he says, gesturing to where he's been leaning in.

"I can smell it from here, asshole."

He stands up. "Asshole is right; that's what it smells like, a filthy asshole. You're no fucking fun. Seriously, though, that smells like sugar-coated shit or something, like a donut shop with a massive sewage back up."

"Well, that's certainly appealing enough to make me reconsider my earlier impulse to decline getting closer to it."

They continue looking through the house, discovering more of the puddles in various rooms but little else out of the ordinary.

"Must have been gone for a little while," he says.

"What makes you say that?"

He gestures to the food dishes laid out on the floor. "No food left for the cats and none of them are hanging around. Open door gave them an invitation to fend for themselves out there, I guess."

"How many cats did she have?" Ren takes note of the number of food dishes and recalls seeing three separate letterboxes during her exploration.

"I'm hazarding a conservative guess of five," he says.

"That's fucking sad," she mutters as she hears their backup pulling up to the curb outside. The lights from the patrol car splash across the walls, making the empty house somehow feel more uncomfortable.

"Well, that was a wash," he says.

"I'm not sure I'm disappointed she isn't here. Something is really not right about this case."

He nods as the newly arrived officers walk in, faces contorted and hands covering noses and mouths.

"Be sure to collect samples from these puddles throughout the house," Ren says, taking charge. "We want to find out what that is."

"I'm going outside to smoke," Martin says.

"I'll join you. I have to get away from this smell."

They walk out to the sidewalk where they share a cigarette, greedily breathing in the smoke, finally overpowering the smell from inside.

Chapter Ten

She had never been the sort of girl who would go home with a stranger. She wasn't even the type who would fuck on the first date. And yet, here she is, fumbling and frantic, her lips and hands all over the man she'd never seen before half an hour ago.

Between the drinks and the excitement, she's feeling dizzy as he leads her into his apartment, and she's grateful that he's taking charge.

In the dim light of the spacious apartment, he guides her into the bedroom. and it's only a moment before she lets herself fall back on the bed. Vision blurry and poorly focused, he is still so handsome, and the bedding smells like him, with the same scent she found so appealing, almost intoxicating, as he'd slid up next to her at the bar.

Laying back, she begins unbuttoning her blouse, fumbling as she focuses on trying to watch as he removes his shirt. It's been some time for her. But there's no excuse for losing track of what she's doing as she squints to see that he's as sculpted as she felt like he'd be when she'd been running her hands all over him during the cab ride here.

Giggling, she returns to the task of undressing herself, unclasping her bra in the front. Feeling the cool air of the room on her nipples makes them harder than they already had been, almost painfully tightening the sensitive skin.

He's standing still now, at the foot of the bed, shirtless and magnificent, watching her hungrily. She lifts her feet onto the bed, raises her hips and slides her skirt and panties down, enjoying the way he silently watches her and feeling admired in a way she hasn't in a long time.

Her feet still planted flat on the bed, she relaxes her legs as her knees separate and her feet slide farther apart. She watches him over the rise of her breasts gazing down at her, framed by her elevated thighs as he begins to undo his jeans.

Even intoxicated and on the dusk side of consciousness, she almost screams as he lurches forward toward her, his penis coming into view.

The best way to describe the man's erection would be to liberally apply the words knobby and malformed. Though everything else about his appearance was perfectly normal, his penis looks like the product of 30 generations of unrepentant inbreeding. It's like something out of a horror story she read when she was a teenager, spreading insanity and terror to any who dared to gaze upon it, and yet she can't make herself look away.

And then it moves.

It isn't an involuntary twitch, or any signal of arousal she'd witnessed before. It moves like a prehensile tail on a monkey, or like a snake.

Like a snake, it strikes as he thrusts himself downward, stifling her attempt to scream with his slavering mouth.

Chapter Eleven

Stephen Lee stares at them over his desk, his expression impassive. "Your report mentioned that the missing woman was a cat owner?"

Not sure where this is going, Martin replies, "Yeah, she probably had half a dozen, maybe more."

"Well," he begins, "I can tell you that they more than likely didn't wander off into the neighborhood as your report suggested."

Neither of them is certain how to interpret what their colleague is saying. They hadn't thought about the cats at all since they'd filled out their reports on the events of that evening.

The ME simply waits while he watches them turning the questions over in their minds, waiting for a sign that one of them has figured it out. He's a little surprised when it's not Ren who reaches the cheese at the center of this maze.

"Oh fuck," he sighs. "Those puddles all over the house?"

"That is correct," he replies. His flat tone makes it clear that this isn't something amusing to him. "Fecal matter, digestive enzymes, and trace amounts of feline fur and bone that hadn't been fully digested."

"Something ate the cats?" Ren doesn't know how else to respond than by questioning it. She doesn't even like cats, and the thought still repulses her.

"Someone," Stephen corrected, "a person did this. It's stronger than usual, more potent, but the digestive acid is human."

"That stuff, whatever we should be calling it," she replies, "it didn't look like shit. Sure, I've seen diarrhea before, but that's not what this was, even though it smelled like it."

"There's a medical condition known as fecal emesis, wherein what a person eats gets blocked up somewhere in the lower digestive tract and everything starts coming back the way it came."

"People can shit from their mouths?" he asks, struggling not to laugh at the absurdity of what he's hearing. "There was a South Park episode like that."

"This is no cartoon, I'm afraid, and fecal emesis is the result of serious medical issues." The ME smirks for a moment, before continuing, "Not the byproduct of shoving food up one's ass."

"This guy gets it!" he blurts out before remembering why they're there.

"So," Ren interrupts, getting the conversation back on track, "she eats her cats, and then vomits the digested remains up all over her house?"

"From where I'm sitting, that's sort of what it looks like. I'm confused about a few things, but one thing in particular. The photos of the scene and your written reports, they don't indicate any sign of blood or anything resembling uneaten remains."

"I definitely didn't see any," Martin replies, and she nods in the affirmation that she hadn't seen anything either.

"Then, ignoring the fact that it is quite impossible, it would seem as if the woman had somehow managed to devour the cats whole."

"Wha..." he begins before the ME cuts him off.

"It gets stranger still," he says as he shuffles through some of the files on his desk. "The headless man from the landfill a few days back, he had traces of a similarly potent digestive acid all over his neck."

"Ok, stop," Ren interrupts him tersely. "I expect this from my idiot of a partner, and his juvenile sense of humor sometimes. I'm not going to sit here while you try to tell me that our missing woman ate a man's head and then vomited the digested remains of her meal onto his neck before depositing him into a dumpster."

"Even I'm having a hard time with this one," Martin adds. "I'm not sure what the punchline here is."

"I wish it was a joke," Stephen says. The stern expression on his face is hinting at resignation. "My job is typically a great deal easier than this, and a lot less confusing."

Chapter Twelve

The autumn clouds cling to the forested mountainside to the Southeast as if they were spawned from the dark green foliage. The low cloud ceiling casts everything in a subdued half-light, reflecting the faint light from Denver, 30 miles away.

These are the early mornings Adam Beckett lives for; the precise sort of conditions he ventures out pre-dawn to capture. The moonlight on the low-hanging clouds lends a sort of fantasy surrealism to the landscape, and the sunrise, still another hour away, will surely be magnificent.

The morning begins to feel all that much more serendipitous as the weathered old barn emerges from the shadows in the field to his left. Trespassing in abandoned buildings isn't the sort of thing he shies away from, and the field surrounding the site doesn't appear to be recently tended.

He carefully scrambles over a battered barbed wire fence into the overgrown field and makes his way to the structure.

He carefully sets his camera gear down and explores the exterior of the barn with his flashlight, not trusting the moon to shed enough light to keep him safe from hazards as he circles the building.

He almost exclaims when he glances up and sees the partially shattered window facing the East. Catching himself, he instead whispers, "Perfect."

Camera gear collected, he makes his way into the dingy and dusty interior of the barn and toward the window he'd seen from the outside. Timing is everything, and he wants to get the shot, figuring he can explore a bit more while he waits for sunrise. The interior of the glass is streaked with dust, and cobwebs stream from the window frame on the faint breeze making its way in. Everything is perfect. Right there, in the space left vacant by the missing pieces of glass, is the full moon.

It takes him a couple of minutes to set up his tripod and adjust the settings on his camera. Satisfied, he takes a few shots, makes some tweaks to ISO, and shoots some more. He reviews what he's gotten, further adjusts his focus, and takes a few more before transitioning to a different lens and going through the same process all over again.

He packs up most of his equipment, leaving it on the dirt floor next to the tripod where he hopes to be as sunrise begins to light up the horizon. Everything will be easy to retrieve as he returns to the field to capture some different shots of the upcoming dawn.

The rear of the cavernous space is walled off, and he imagines once-upon-a-time it served as more of a livestock holding area rather than the garage-like space he's currently in. He shoves on the sliding door and picks up a strange combination of odors as he struggles to force the heavy wooden panel along its neglected groove. There is dust and soil, for sure, but there's also something alkaline, and a sweetness that reminds him of meat left unrefrigerated and forgotten.

Adam's flashlight cuts through the gloom and falls to the floor as his fingers lose their grip. He doesn't scream. He tries to, but he has no breath with which he could do so. He fumbles on the ground for the fallen flashlight, unable to look away from what's in front of him, unable to process exactly what he's seeing.

He backs away and pulls his phone from the pocket where it's tucked away.

No signal.

He turns and runs from the barn, forgetting his camera equipment and forgetting the sunrise that had been so important to him. He follows the rutted dirt and gravel road from the dilapidated farm, desperately hoping for a signal, and terrified of what could be lurking around him in the dark.

He's run a full half-mile before he can dial 9-11, and he has to catch his hitching breath as he tries to explain where he is, and what he's seen.

He sounds unhinged to his own ears as he babbles to the disembodied voice over the phone. What he saw in the barn was the product of insanity, and maybe he's been touched by it now. He certainly feels lost when the distant sirens finally intrude on the stillness of the morning.

"Took you long enough," Ren shouts as she approaches his car. "Did your GPS fail or something?"

Slamming his door in irritation, Martin gestures around them with his hands, taking in the whole surrounding environment. "What the fuck are we doing way out here in the boonies?"

"Sheriff's department asked that we come out here because of some of the things we've been running into back in the city."

He sighs, knowing the answer before he asks the question. "You're talking about that weird shit, aren't you?"

She nods, her eyes displaying the same exasperation he's been feeling.

"Well, may as well rip the bandage right off. What are we dealing with?"

"No idea, yet," she replies. "I was waiting for you to show up before I got myself formally introduced to the locals."

The sheriff introduces himself to them and points to a nearby squad car, directing them to the photographer who had called the police from a couple of miles down the road. He attempts to prepare them for what they're going to see inside of the barn, but he stumbles over every attempt to describe the scene. They assure him that they'll get acquainted with the environment for themselves. The man's unguarded expression lays bare relief that he doesn't have to describe the scene inside.

A handful of deputies come and go as they make their way to the open barn doors, carrying on with the tasks set before them, and the farm has become more active than it more than likely had been for years, Ren thinks. When they enter, she realizes there's been something going on here for a while now. As her eyes adjust to the relative darkness inside, she can hardly tell the difference where machines end and humans begin.

The sheriff may have attempted to describe this to them, but it wouldn't have prepared them for what they're seeing. They slowly move through the intervening space, approaching the focal point of the crime scene, while wanting to do nothing more than turn around and walk away.

"Kinda reminds me of 4-H," he mutters under his breath as he examines the machinery.

"What the fuck?" Ren asks, shaking her head incredulously at what she just heard. "You're going to need to explain that one a little bit."

He smiles slightly, not expecting her to have heard him. "I grew up outside of the city, you know."

"That really doesn't explain anything."

Still absently staring at the interior of the barn, he continues. "My grandparents were farmers, and 4-H was just one of those things that farming and ranching kids participated in."

He meanders over and begins fiddling with the apparatus,

careful to avoid touching the penis or the corpse still attached to it. "This," he gestures, "looks like it was modified from the same sort of equipment ranchers use on dairy farms for milking their cows."

Reaching around behind the cadaver, he touches the piston that is still inserted into the man's anal cavity. "This," he begins, "as best I can tell, is being used to stimulate the prostate to force ejaculation"

"So, you're suggesting..."

"Yup, I'm pretty certain these men were being milked for their semen," he says, shivering as he finishes the statement.

They continue looking around the facility, the deputies making way for them to analyze the setup.

"We'll have to wait until everything has been tested," he says, "but I am positive that some of these IV feeds are filled with narcotics of some kind, and the others are to keep the men hydrated."

One of the local deputies speaks up from where he's examining the scene, "You're exactly right. This equipment in here is nothing more than crudely modified milking pumps, just like the kind we use with dairy cows." He pauses for a moment before continuing, "These are antiques, for sure, but the principle is still the same."

"Let me get this straight," she says, gesturing toward the nearest body. "Someone was milking these men?"

The two men look at one another pointedly for a moment before Martin replies, "That's sure as shit what it looks like to me."

The deputy offers a grim nod before looking away and returning to what he was doing. Suddenly uncomfortable with the attention he's drawn to himself and feeling something akin to shame under her gaze.

She looks around the surroundings, evaluating the scene with the new information at the front of her mind. The rusted machinery begins to appear progressively more sinister and disorienting, the desiccated men pinioned amid the equipment looking like mummies uncovered by some far off in the future archaeologists.

Unaware of it, her face takes on a grimace the longer she peruses the surroundings; the horror of it all sinks deep into her.

He makes her jump just slightly as he gently places his hand on her shoulder, "Are you all right?"

Shaking her head in the vain attempt to dispel the horror she's feeling, she says, "I don't know if alright will ever be accurate with something like this."

"I've been thinking the same thing," he replies. "None of this makes any sense at all and it only seems to be getting worse with every new call we get dragged out on."

She nods in response, with no words to utter that might help. She focuses on the machinery, trying to wrap her head around how someone would arrange something like this, and why anyone would want to.

In addition to the half dozen desiccated men still connected to the equipment, two times that number had been located in a shallow mass grave dug out inside of a stall that once held cattle. Eighteen victims, with no rhyme nor reason associated with their apparent selection beyond the fact that they are all men.

Martin isn't masking his discomfort sufficiently for her not to see right through. Crimes with an obvious sexual component like these always hit him harder than the more straightforward variety; they hit her harder as well.

This one is different for him, though, as the victims happen to be men. That part is abnormal. Most human trafficking and unlawful imprisonment cases involve women or children.

"At least they're adults," he mutters as he's examining the men still attached to the pumps. "Barely, though, in some cases. It's hard to tell with them being all dried out and looking like husks."

"You were right. It's definitely more of the weird shit," she says. "There's no fucking connection, though, aside from the fact that the circumstances make absolutely no fucking sense."

He looks up from where he's kneeling next to the empty IV bag connected to one of the men by stained rubber tubing, "You're right. There's no proximity relationship, the previous victims had nothing in common beyond a place of employment for two of them, but these guys aren't missing from there, and the method is entirely disconnected."

"It doesn't make any fucking sense," she repeats to herself. Her tone of voice is flat, but he can hear the exasperation beneath the surface. He knows her too well for it to go unnoticed.

"The world we live in, I guess," he replies. "Maybe it's just a weird fluke, like a real-life version of the full moon nonsense you hear about from television and whatnot."

"Maybe," she mutters, before trailing off.

It takes hours for the site to be processed and the bodies to be extracted, both from the apparatus and from where they'd been casually tossed into the hole in the earth, and fed into their respective body bags. They remain at the scene through it all, assessing everything, separately and together, hoping to find anything that might make sense of the madness here.

As the afternoon wears on, Martin finds himself sitting halfway in the driver's seat of his car as he reads through the transcript of the statement taken from the photographer by the dome light, but there's nothing useful in the report no matter how many times he reads through it.

"There's nothing more for us to do here," she says, interrupting his fourth review of the report.

"You're not wrong," he replies. "We're going to be waiting to find out what was in those IV bags before we maybe have something to work with."

"Meet you at your place?" She asks. She tries to shrug off the frustration and discomfort of the day's investigation to smile what she hopes is a reassuring and seductive smile.

"Of course," he says with a forced grin.

Neither of them can shake the disturbance they feel, but they're both hoping to distract themselves and one another however they can.

The photographer stammers and shivers through his recitation of the events in the barn when he'd discovered the mechanical abattoir. They both know he's innocent, and that he isn't involved in what had happened here, but they are hoping he might have picked up on some detail before the police arrived on site.

His fourth time repeating himself, clarifying things at their prompts, it becomes obvious they aren't going to get anything new.

"You can go home now," Ren says softly, standing up from her seat. "Your belongings can be collected at the front desk."

Adam nods his head and prepares to leave, looking like a shell of a person, drained and emptied.

She extends her hand to him with her card between her index finger and thumb. "My email address is on the card. If you would send me copies of your photos taken in or near the barn, we would appreciate it."

The young man swallows, for the first time thinking about what had drawn him into the barn in the first place as something not just in the past. "I can do that this evening," he assures her, and he walks through the door.

"That poor kid is going to be fucked up for a long time," Martin observes.

She sits back down, staring blankly at the surface of the table for a moment. "I think we're well on our way to being all sorts of fucked up as well."

He considers arguing for a moment, but knows it would be futile and dishonest. "I guess maybe it's a good thing we're already fucked."

She chuckles half-heartedly. "I sometimes hate it when you're right."

"That would explain why you're always so filled with hate."

"Fuck you," she snorts."Let's head down to the cooler and see how the ME is doing with some of these."

"Sounds like a plan."

Adam downloads the photos from his camera and onto the computer as soon as he gets home As he'd told the detectives he would, he emails the photos from the early morning hours.

The photos he captured through the cobwebbed, broken window turn out as haunting and as beautiful as he'd imagined, without any editing involved. It's a relief that he doesn't need to do so, because he can't bear to look at them for more than a moment. He is haunted, less by the images than by the things he saw after capturing the shots. Fragmentary moments from that traumatizing experience are already forcing their way into his mind unbidden. He can think of no reason to intentionally subject himself to that kind of torture.

Therapy sessions take the edge off over the following months, but no amount of professional care helps him cope with what he feels each time he comes across a photo from that day. He would have deleted them right away, but he couldn't bring himself to erase some of the most beautiful shots he'd ever taken. He holds out hope that he will someday be able to view those images without being inundated with the horror that naturally follows.

He retains that hope right up to the day he takes his own life, two years after that horrible morning. He doesn't even admit it to himself, but the antecedent to his suicide is a few seconds of news broadcast where a video shows black and white spotted cows on a dairy farm. Just a handful of frames of video display those cows in a barn, quite dissimilar to the run down one he remembers, hooked up to milking equipment.

Chapter Thirteen

Missing persons cases have always been more common than most people suspect, especially in major cities. It is a sad fact that law enforcement has always been well aware of. Many times the individual turns out not to have been missing at all, but the remaining number is always a staggering thing to consider.

Here in Denver, as in most larger metropolitan areas, they also maintain records of missing persons amongst the homeless population. There is always a larger margin of error in tabulating actual numbers within the transients of the city, but recently an alarming surge in people disappearing from the streets, as well as the population at large, has helped to isolate some specific target regions for greater police presence.

Obsessed with making some sort of connection between the various aberrant crimes they've been investigating, Martin insists that they spend their downtime cruising through these areas of greater activity. She can't even formulate an argument against the plan, because she feels a similar need to finally put the pieces together into some sort of pattern. She can't think of a better way to invest their time than aimlessly driving through some of the worst neighborhoods they can find. It's been the same routine for three days.

"You can feel it out there," he says, breaking the silence. "The tension and the fear. It's in the air."

Ren hates to agree with him, but she can feel it too. She can see the furtive glances from people as they cross the gaps of alleyways, people catching themselves peering into the shadows clearly afraid of what they might see.

"Fewer people on the sidewalks, for sure," she confirms.

"They know something is off, even if they can't put a name to it," he says. "It isn't just the increased police presence either, though I bet that has cemented it for some of them."

"Four of the victims from the barn contraption were taken from this same section of a few blocks, so I'd be surprised if some of the residents didn't know them or their families."

He stares out the window for a few minutes, the buildings and traffic blurring together beyond his point of focus, lost in thought again. The occasional burst of static and brief commentary over the radio are the only sounds now that he's gone quiet.

"It's more than that, though, I think," he finally says after a couple of minutes. "Sure, we're a bit more in the loop, being the ones stuck investigating this shit, but regardless of that, you can feel it too, like something is wrong at a deeper level."

She's almost afraid to respond, knowing exactly what he's talking about but not wanting to lend it her voice of assent. Instead, she chooses to query him, keeping her tone innocent and steady, "What do you mean?"

"Fuck. I don't know how to put it into words. It's like something is seeping up from the basement and through the floorboards, an unusual noise or an odor, you know, like the heartbeat from The Tell-Tale Heart, if the world happened to be the house in my analogy."

She remains silent, contemplating his words.

"That sounded really stupid," he says nervously, suddenly feeling like he made an ass of himself. "You do know what I mean, though, right?"

She nods slowly and he sees the gesture from the corner of his left eye. His heart rate immediately decreases, relieved that he might not have sounded quite as much like an idiot as he'd worried he had.

The rest of the day goes on as uneventfully as the previous two days had, but the discomfort and tension only seem to be worse now that they've acknowledged it.

She goes home with him that evening and stays the night, knowing that she's only fueling his future arguments that she should move in with him. She halfway wonders if it might be better to remain close to one another. The events of the previous month have been taking a toll on her even though she masks it better than he does.

Chapter Fourteen

Laying in bed, torn between his need for sleep and his fear of the nightmares that might follow him from the waking world and into his dreams, he starts thinking about a different strip club from a few years before. The two of them had just met when they'd initially been assigned to work together.

He recalled quite clearly, the first case they'd worked, and it felt like it was a different life and a different world back then. That first case, a nightmarish one, somehow seemed to set the stage for everything that they'd been dealing with since.

The sign outside had advertised Live Nude Girls in garish neon, and that evening it was less than honest. The tableau before them was ghastly, to say the least. The bodies of the girls were draped in all manner of lewd positions upon the stage without a single shred of cloth between them to spare a trace of dignity. The wounds had been left untended, and the tacky brownish fluid which had all too recently been red had spilled from the edge of the stage to the floor below by the time they'd arrived on the scene.

Everything about what they'd seen that night was terrible, and yet he realized he would gladly return to the relative sanity of a crime scene like that if it meant he could avoid any more of these strange fucking cases.

The crime was horrific, and it was strange in its cruelty, the way any act of brutality was strange to a sane person. Looking back, he sort of wonders if the girls on that first case were the lucky ones; their ends had been quick compared to what he'd been seeing recently. It was straightforward violence perpetrated by a sick fuck with anger issues and no capacity to accept rejection with anything resembling grace.

If they ultimately find a motive behind this current batch of murders that is anywhere near that banal, he will be so shocked he might end up hospitalized. It won't be so cut and dried this time, he does not doubt. That man's impetus may have been unrelatable to him, but it was something he and his partner could wrap their heads around without extensive mental gymnastics involved.

He dispels the memories of those long-dead girls' faces with some effort, and he rolls his head just slightly on his pillow to watch Ren sleep, her back draped in shadows that make her appear even darker, almost black. She always sleeps better than he does, and less fitfully. His difficulty sleeping seems to be getting worse lately, even though she stays the night more often. He enjoys watching her sleep, though; it doesn't bother him when she's asleep while he's battling insomnia.

He wakes from another nightmare, careful not to disturb Ren who still sleeps soundly beside him. He manages to get his breathing under control with exercises he learned as a child, and his heart rate follows suit.

Shit is getting spooky out there, he thinks to himself. These investigations are getting to him and, as much as he tries to pass things off as some big, cosmic joke, it is getting under his skin.

Skull, flesh, and brain ate away by digestive acids, cannibal arsonists, and men being milked for semen; these simply aren't the sorts of things he could have prepared for. Everything is starting to get surreal in a big way, and it is impacting his sleep horribly.

He can't even recall any specifics of the most recent dream. It's a blur of half-recollected images and sensations, but it was bad enough that he'd been pulled awake.

He takes comfort in Ren's presence, though he can't understand how she can be so seemingly untroubled by the way things have been going.

For her sake, in an attempt to avoid waking her, he decides to remain in bed. It's a slow process, but he does finally calm himself and make his way back to sleep.

Chapter Fifteen

It's the second week of their patrols of the most impacted neighborhoods before they finally encounter something out of the ordinary. Even as insistent as he is that these neighborhoods are where they belong, he would have suggested they were wasting their time had it not been for the disappearances remaining well above average. Spikes in those numbers appeared in an expanding radius around the affected locations.

"Stop!"

Ren doesn't hesitate to brake hard, and her head swivels the direction her partner's pointing before the sedan has reached a complete stop.

The form in the alley is difficult to make out with the building still in the way of the sun on the other side, but she understands immediately what drew Martin's attention as they'd driven past. Something just appears wrong with what she's able to make out.

Out of the shadows, one figure stands and begins bolting down the alley before she is even off of the radio and opening the door. Martin's slightly faster, but has to circle the front end of the car on his way to the alley entrance.

The running figure suddenly drops out of view, and they both speed forward, alarmed and perplexed.

Ren glances down as they pass the unmoving figure lying still on the pavement. It could be the shade of the route they're taking, but she is almost certain the prone individual doesn't have an exposed bit of flesh that isn't purple with bruising and swelling. The glimpse brings to mind photos she recalls seeing of affected areas in cases of rattlesnake bites.

They stop sharply as they see how the runner disappeared.

"We're going down there after him aren't we?" he asks.

She replies, "We absolutely are!"

"Backup on the way?"

She nods her affirmation as she swings her legs down into the gaping hole and lowers herself down into the sewer.

She waits to reach the ground before pulling out her flashlight to swing it in both directions. The unnatural stillness delays her reaction as the light slides over a filthy young man whose silhouette looks a lot like the runner above ground. It isn't until they're both down and aiming their lights at him that she speaks, "Stay where you are," she says, managing to project her voice without sounding like she's yelling.

The young man doesn't respond, continuing to stare at them without any expression on his face.

As they begin to cross the twenty feet or so separating them from their quarry, he shoots off down the tunnel, racing away from them.

"God damn it," he shouts as they begin pursuit.

They both keep themselves in good shape, but they keep losing ground because of the boy's pace. They follow him down curving sewer lines and branching arteries, but he knows the territory, not hesitating or slowing down at all and consistently increasing his lead. He's getting too far ahead of them and they have to slow down, holding their breath as they reach new intersections to pick up the faint sounds of his escape. Even his footfalls are largely silent, and neither of them can hear anything over the sound of blood rushing through their veins.

Of course, the tunnel would have to branch off in two directions after they've already stumbled through sewage and filth for five minutes, chasing after the first possible suspect they've found. They sweep their flashlights around, cones of illumination slicing through the darkness, but providing no helpful clues to discern which route their suspect had fled. Everything in the gloom looks the same.

Standing still and listening intently for any sound that might give away the correct path, they both struggle to still their labored breathing. He finally speaks up, having heard nothing that points them the direction of their prey, "I'll take the right. You go left. If you find this little fucker, fire off a warning round, and I will turn back. I'll do the same if I see him."

She nods. "Good luck," she says, and she begins a splashing jog down the tunnel to the left without any further hesitation, the circle of light bobbing and dancing around ahead of her. He watches her disappear into the blackness and feels an immediate sense of loss and dread as he turns and makes his way down the opposite tunnel.

It feels claustrophobic to him in a way it hadn't when his partner had been beside him. Shadows appear to be taking on a new life, one hostile and threatening. Even though he knows it's just his nerves getting to him, his heart races more than the exertion would merit.

The depressing sameness of everything makes him feel like he's making no progress and any hope that he's on the killer's trail fades with each step.

Ren is feeling the same, aside from the claustrophobia. Somehow, she's becoming certain, they had lost the little fucker. By now there should be a large police presence at street level where the partially devoured body remains, and some officers should be down here as well, coming in as backup, but she has no idea how far they've traveled since following the cannibal down into the sewer.

At least he can't go back the way he came, she thinks to herself, finding a modicum of solace in that.

She's beginning to tire and is actively considering turning back when she hears the echoing report of gunfire.

"Gotcha, fucker!" She mutters as she picks up her pace back the direction she came, to find her partner and hopefully finally find some fucking answers.

Martin had almost missed the suspect's presence right in front of him because there was no reason for him to expect to find him clinging to the ceiling of the tunnel. Even seeing him when he did, he had no time to react as the suspect dropped down and knocked him into the water.

He was immediately dragged along the tunnel, roughly knocked about by the rapid pace.

He holds tight to his firearm and flashlight, with the rapid strobing of the light on the walls of the tunnel as disorienting as the motion of being dragged through the filthy water.

It isn't instantly apparent that he's stopped and that the pressure of the hand gripping his ankle is no longer present, but he jumps to his feet, sweeping his light around the new space he finds himself standing in.

There are five of them circling him in this relatively open space, each one identical and identically horrific in appearance, and he has to turn his eyes away from a couple at any given moment to catch a glimpse of the others. Circling in place, he struggles to remain calm.

They look like children, barely adolescent, grimy and coated in filth. Tattered and stained clothing hang from emaciated forms. The eyes are hateful and mean, like the eyes of every schoolyard bully he'd ever seen.

It's the fucking mouths, though, that make him uncomfortable. Hanging open, each of the boys has a mouth filled with jagged, elongated, uneven teeth. He's not even certain the mouths could properly close without the protuberances grinding harshly against each other.

He desperately tries to make sense of the scene as he spins slowly around, taking in every detail no matter how challenging it is to absorb.

Suddenly one of them lunges from his blind spot and sinks jagged teeth into his left forearm.

He squeezes the trigger by reflex, his lack of sleep taking its toll, and the round penetrates the abdomen of the strange boy standing in front of him.

A harsh, deafening scream bursts out of the nightmare mouths of the boys and he drops his gun. His hands reach to cover his ears. Tears form in his eyes, and through the watery haze, he sees the boys coming together in a group in front of him, standing side-by-side, with the injured one in the center.

After what feels like forever, the screeching subsides. They return to staring at him, angrier and more hate-filled than they had previously appeared.

Whatever these things are, they aren't human. Seeing them side-by-side as they were, it was obvious that they were identical. He isn't even sure that identical quintuplets are a thing, but these fucking things aren't normal children. He knows that much for sure.

"What are you?"

They simply continue glaring at him, offering no answer to his question.

"Do you understand me?"

Still no response forthcoming, they retain the same expression.

When they finally speak, he almost screams, as all of them open their mouths at the same time. "We are the end of you."

Not knowing how to process that answer, he figures they're

fucking with him somehow.

"Where the fuck did you come from?" he asks, begging his voice to remain steadier than his nerves.

"We slithered and squirmed our way into your world like maggots." The words arise from all five of the boys as one, each mouth moving in unison. "And like maggots, we became flies in search of rot and filth. We found hosts, and we laid our eggs within their flesh to be reborn in this world."

The voices stop as he recovers his 9mm from where he'd dropped it to the ground.

They watch him with curiosity and no apparent fear before they continue speaking. "In these bodies, we found our new forms and burst forth like a flood. Only a few dozen of us stumbled across the breach into your world, but others will surely come. Your time here is short, and we will take your place."

"What do you want with our world?"

"We were forgotten by you, and left to starve. We will starve no more. We want to feed. We want to consume. You will all be consumed, and when you are gone, we will find another world after this one is a husk, and we will devour that world, as well. This is what we are. This is what we do."

Just as all of the voices had spoken as one, they all become silent again. Mouths filled with jagged teeth, like shards of sheared metal and broken glass hang open, slack and drooling with ravenous hunger.

He backs slowly away, the heads of his audience swiveling to follow, the eyes cruel and focused with casual disdain. He knows that they will swarm over him and swallow him piece by piece until nothing is left; he just doesn't know why they haven't already. He doubts it's the gun, though they know it can hurt them, because there's no way he can shoot all five of them before they are on him.

Tense moments pass as he waits for the inevitable surge. When they do finally move, he fires almost out of reflex. Instead of coming at him, they are moving closer to each other, shoulder-to-shoulder, and arm-to-arm, they cluster together. The shaking and vibrating are difficult to recognize for what it is at first; he initially suspects it's simply the wavering light from his flashlight.

What happens next is harder for him to dismiss, and mentally processing the scene almost breaks his already strained mind.

The shaking in front of him becomes more violent and severe, and the separation between one of the things in front of him and those next to it is disappearing. They aren't simply getting closer to one another, they are combining.

A wet, crunching noise intrudes over the sounds of the sewer he'd been hearing, and he stifles gagging that threatens to erupt his stomach contents.

The process continues, becoming more disorienting by the moment, and he would question his sobriety if he wasn't all too familiar with how numerous substances feel. He questions his sanity as the five creatures become one amorphous, shuddering mass of flesh and organs; he knows, as crazy as it seems, this is real.

Familiar looking limbs and features emerge and dissolve back into the writhing monstrosity, and before it can find a new shape, he knows that he has to leave. He has to at least try.

He exhales as calmly as he can manage and presses against the trigger repeatedly with the barrel aimed as near the center of this thing as he can manage.

While the blasts echo down the concrete walls around him, he turns and runs as fast as his sore legs will propel him back the way he'd come.

He doesn't hear it coming his way, but he doesn't dare take his eyes off of the path ahead of him for fear of getting lost. He doesn't even know what its pursuit would sound like if it is hunting him down. He's certain he'll find out as it catches up to him.

Chapter Sixteen

"I don't know what the hell I'm supposed to do at this point," Martin says. "This whole thing still feels ridiculously unreal. I thought sleeping on it might help clear things up."

Still groggy from sleep, Ren replies, "That makes two of us, because I am at a total loss as far as how we move forward from here."

Normally he would be aware that Ren is going to speak, but he's lost in his thoughts and unaware of his surroundings to a large extent.

"Have you thought about what it said to you down there?"

He chuckles momentarily, with no humor to the noise, and cracks a grin that looks more grimace than an expression of amusement. "I've thought of very little else since I came back up aboveground yesterday."

She'd figured that to be the case. He was shaken in a way she'd never seen and he had remained distant and disengaged the whole day, except when he'd taken the time to describe what he'd seen and heard down in the sewer. The version of events she'd heard for the second time this evening had been unedited, quite dissimilar to the abridged statement that had gone into the paperwork.

She holds his faraway gaze. "Do you think it's real? What it was saying?"

"I think we're in real fucking trouble," he replies, "because what I saw down there made me a believer."

Silence uncomfortably takes hold of the room, and neither of them can think of anything to say in response to that. It's out in the open now. Being honest with herself, she is starting to believe as well. She has known him for years and never known him to embellish or let his imagination get away from him. The shit he'd shared scared the fuck out of her, and it explained some of the weirder things they'd been seeing in the field.

Sitting there in the living room, she shudders as she considers the implications for the first time. In the silence, he shivers as well, as similar thoughts crawl through his mind, as they had been the whole evening.

After a lengthy discussion, they decide that they should run all of the new information past the medical examiner. Of all the possibilities, he seems the most likely to hear them out without writing it all off as insanity or some perverse practical joke. She may not have witnessed it for herself, but she believes his description of the encounter down in the sewer the day before without hesitation. Had they not witnessed so many other thoroughly lunatic situations leading up to the horror down there, she may still have believed him. The shared experiences, however, served to speed that conclusion.

The ME is the only other person they worked with who might be able to connect the dots and make some sort of sense of what was utter nonsense to them no matter how many times they attempted to wrap their heads around things. It was a long shot, but it was also their only shot at finding some solution.

"The worst thing that could happen is that he might laugh us out of his office," she says with what she hopes is a comforting tone of voice that might compensate for what she knows is a forced smile.

"No," he replies tersely. "The worst thing that could happen is that he can go to the chief and report this wild tale. At that point, there will be investigations and mandatory drug tests that we will both undoubtedly fail."

She hesitates for a minute before responding to his admittedly reasonable concern. "So," she asks patiently, "what would you like to do?"

"Well, there isn't anything else to do. We have to take this to him," he says, sounding both sullen and resigned in a way that makes her want to embrace him and slap him at the same time. "I just wanted to be realistic about what the outcome very well could be."

"Asshole."

He chuckles half-heartedly, and she can't help but join him.

Chapter Seventeen

Overflowing with nervous energy, Martin begins rattling off the whole story of what they'd experienced after following the suspect into the sewers the day before. He includes all the details he'd left out of the official report. The words pour out as the impulse to shut up and run away is suppressed by the momentum of the telling itself.

He also starts sharing little details about some of the recent cases that had been dismissed by him at the time, surprising both himself and his partner at just how long he keeps going.

Through it all, their colleague remains silent and impassive. As skilled as she is with reading people, the man remains a fucking cipher even after Martin finally stops speaking half an hour later.

"Don't get me wrong," the Medical Examiner finally says after a painfully protracted silence. "Some part of me wants to laugh hysterically before tossing the two of you out of my office."

Both of them feel immediately disheartened. Neither are as confident as they had been when the conversation started, and they weren't entirely confident then.

"But," he begins, before either of them can protest, a strange tone evident in the word, "I have been seeing some strange results coming back on tests I've been requesting, and a lot of other things haven't been coming together in a way that fits with anything I'd expect. This admittedly batshit crazy tale that you've been spinning." He pauses, pointedly looking at both of them, almost begging them to confirm that it's all been a joke. "Well, it certainly makes more sense than assuming the lab techs are pulling off some kind of prank on me. There's no good reason for it, and, quite frankly, I doubt they have the imagination to pull off something this elaborate."

"What results are you talking about?" She asks, feeling relieved for the first time since the decision was made to come into the office, but also feeling apprehensive about what she's about to hear.

"Let's start with the toxicology screening from your apparent arson victim," he begins, pulling up some data on his laptop. "There were trace chemical compounds in his lungs that we know didn't come from the fire due to his clearly being deceased before ignition took place, but also because no fuel I can think of would produce anything like these chemicals. Even if the victim had spent a substantial period alive and breathing in the smoke, I would have serious questions regarding what was burning."

Stephen trails off for a minute, trying to think of what he's supposed to say next. Lost in thought, he loses track of time as the patience of his audience of two steadily evaporates.

"And?" She finally replies after the silence stretches out too far.

He shakes his head, clearing his thoughts. "Sorry," he replies, "I was trying to figure out a way to explain the findings in layman's terms."

"We're not stupid, asshole," Martin says with a chuckle. "Well, she's not," he adds as a correction.

"I'm not suggesting either of you are stupid, just that I want my explanation to be clear," he explains.

Another few seconds of silence insinuate themselves into the growing tension in the room before he speaks again. "The chemicals in our victim's lungs bear a strong resemblance to two compounds you're both, I'm sure, familiar with. The first is extremely close to MDMA, closer to it than methamphetamine is. The second is barely discernible from the active chemicals in Viagra."

The two partners look at one another, feeling as confused as the Medical Examiner.

Ren looks back to Stephen, "So, our crispy victim was downing Ecstasy and Viagra?"

"That's incorrect," he replies. "He wasn't popping pills at all. This residue was in his lungs, not his stomach contents. He was breathing it in, inhaling it, and with absurd potency based on what we could get from his blood." Stephen pauses for a moment before continuing. "What's extraordinary is how fast these substances are being metabolized. These substances, as similar as they might be to the drugs they resemble, have a drastically diminished half-life. I suspect that's why the substances weren't showing up on some of the earlier tests, or at least registering with such minimal nanogram measurements as to seem irrelevant."

"So," Martin interrupts, "I don't suppose you're going to suggest anything as simple as the possibility that the dead man was snorting lines of ecstasy and Viagra before working up a massive sweat during sex?"

"As crazy as that would be, the truth is far more peculiar," he replies. "His sinus cavities, throat, and lungs, as well as the inside of his mouth, are telling us a very different story. From what I can glean, he was breathing it in as something sublimated, gaseous, in the air."

"I suspect you don't mean he was smoking it somehow," Martin responds, knowing it's exactly what he's about to hear.

"You're right on the money. The closest I can come to hazarding a guess is that it's somehow aerosolized." He pauses and frowns.

"It's about to get more bizarre, though, because the same sort of chemical mixture was in those IVs from the barn the other day, suspended along with the expected fluids and nutrients."

"What?" she asks, finally having the connection they had been searching for.

"You heard me correctly," he says with a grim smile. "The problem is that these chemicals aren't what you'd buy if you went searching for them. I found evidence that points to these variations as being biological, like how you produce pheromones and some frogs sweat poison. That little detail changes everything."

"I pride myself on being a smart man," Stephen says. "I always adapted well in medical school, and I've never stopped learning and expanding my expertise. Over the years I've spent doing this job, I have encountered things that forced me to heavily adjust my perspective and learn new things. What we are seeing here, with this rash of recent deaths, it has me feeling out of my depth."

"That doesn't instill much confidence," Ren replies sadly.

"Don't I know it," he says. "I wish I could say something that would make you two feel better. I wish I could make myself feel more comfortable about any of this. All three of us know that all of these cases are connected, but we couldn't begin to explain those connections to anyone else. Not in any sort of satisfactory manner, at least."

He stands up from his desk and begins pacing around the room, his hard soles tapping against the linoleum as he walks back and forth.

"Especially if we include your story about what happened in the sewer. We could end up being locked away somewhere with white, padded walls. We're all close enough to every stage of these investigations that we can plainly see the way it all fits together better than anyone else would, but it's still as much instinct and gut feeling as anything intellectual or quantifiable."

Ren mulls his words over for a few seconds before replying, "So, what do you suggest?"

Martin speaks before the ME can respond, "We keep our mouths shut and wait for the end of the world, I think is what he's saying."

"It's a bit more nihilistic and grim than I would have put it, but that's about the long and short of it. We'll remain vigilant and conscious of new connections as they appear, we'll investigate everything thoroughly, and, most important, we will be careful. If that thing in the sewer was telling the truth, these things are all over the place and I don't know how we could track all of them down or tell them apart from anyone else on the street."

"And you called me grim," Martin replies.

"We can hopefully catch a break," Ren says. "Something might come along that connects all of the dots in a way that we can take up the chain. Might still look like lunatics, but evidence is evidence."

"Keep your eyes open until then, and keep me in the loop," Stephen says. "I need to understand this. I don't know if understanding will make me any less afraid, but I have to believe that it will."

Stepping out into the night, the shadows feel alive and sinister in a way they never had before. The echoes of a distant car door slamming shut are nearly enough to make them both jump. The conversation with their friend and colleague had gotten under the skin, deeper and with more jagged barbs than either of them had expected.

"There's no coming back from accepting that this is really happening, is there?"

She glances over at him with a trace of additional moisture in her eyes, "I don't think so."

He nods thoughtfully, "This is probably going to be the end, I think."

"You're probably right. That's the feeling I can't shake."

He shuffles his feet on the walk to her car, kicking at loose bits of gravel on the pavement, staring into the mid-distance. The sky glows briefly near the horizon as lightning from a coming storm pierces through the clouds. "Looks like rain tonight," he observes.

"Yup," she says as she glances toward the strobing in the faraway night sky.

She unlocks the car, and they climb inside. Her hand shakes as she places the key into the ignition.

Reaching across the center console, he pats her thigh in what he believes should come across as a reassuring manner. He leaves his hand there for a few seconds longer, lost in his thoughts.

"Fuck it," he finally says. "Let's try to kill some of these bastards before they wipe us out altogether. We can have some fun on the way out and make them work just a bit harder to take our home."

She surprises herself with the impulsive laugh that erupts from her lips. "You're kidding, right? That one you shot just kept coming."

He waits for her laughter to stop, not even feeling chagrined. "It didn't catch me, though."

"It was a giant, misshapen mass of limbs and flesh." Ren still has a difficult time conceiving of the thing Martin described. "It probably only stopped once it got close enough to tell there were more officers down there with us near the sewer entrance. You said it yourself, it didn't drop when you shot it."

He reaches up to her cheek and locks his eyes on her own. "I hurt the fucker. It bled. You've seen Predator before. If it bleeds, we can kill it."

She has to admit that he's making just a little sense, once she's done stifling the smirk that reflexively strives to paint itself across her face.

"Ok," she replies. "Let's put a plan together. Not tonight, though."

The engine turns over and they exit the parking lot as the first drops of rain begin to splash against the pavement. They both know how dangerous hope can be, but they feel the first stirring of that primal emotion as they drive just the same.

Neither of them catches the streetlights reflecting from a dozen eyes crudely organized in a single face watching them from the gutter at the edge of the parking lot as they drive away.

Chapter Eighteen

Finally settled into Martin's apartment, sitting side-by-side on the sofa, neither of them could even consider eating anything for dinner. For all their bluster after their meeting with the ME, it had taken a lot out of both of them.

The television is turned on, but no one is watching. It's serving as nothing more than background noise.

Minutes pass with no sound but their breathing before Martin finally speaks up, and the sound of his voice almost startles her. "Is this the end of the world?"

"Shit, hun. I have no idea," she replies. "It sure seems to be a good fit, though. I can't believe I'm about to say something this fucking stupid, but do you suppose they really are demons or something like that?"

"I've been thinking about that," he says before trailing off.

"Well?"

He shifts in his seat to better look at her. "I've been replaying the whole conversation in my head over and over again, and there wasn't any hint of the religious sort of tirade you'd expect." He pauses for a moment and smiles the closest she's seen to a sincere smile all day. "Or, and this is a real possibility, maybe I've just seen too many movies and my expectations are influenced by Hollywood as far as what I should expect from a demon."

"Fuck," she says. "You have a point. How would we even know anything? Do we need to track down an exorcist or some wizened old priest?"

"Demons or not, I can tell you," he says, "it seems like we're sort of fucked here."

"More than sort of, I'd say."

He nods, and they return to silence. Neither of them has anything more to add as nihilism sinks in. For years, as partners and sometimes lovers, they had established a reputation for gallows humor and remaining unfazed by anything. They had gone through experiences that would have shattered many of their peers, but they had finally reached their crucible.

Separately, they both feel the sense of futility in fighting whatever this is.

They retire to his bedroom and fall asleep without any further conversation. For all of the nameless terror they have been feeling, their sleep is surprisingly untroubled.

The nightmares are outside now, and there's no room left for them in dreams.

ABOUT THE AUTHOR

Nikolas P. Robinson lives in the Black Hills of South Dakota with his girlfriend, his daughter, three dogs, and a cat he's allergic to.

In addition to being a writer, he's a freelance photographer and a lover of the outdoors. His blog can be located at meltdownmessiah.wordpress.com and he can be found on social media platforms as @MeltdownMessiah

If you've enjoyed this, check out these books from

Madness Heart Press

All Men Are Trash by Gina Ranalli

Extinction Peak by Lucas Mangum

Broken Nails by Susan Snyder

In the Beginning by Reed Alexander

Land Shark by Alex Gonzalez

The Reattachment by Doug Ford

A Baptism for the Dead by Charles Bernard

Made in the USA
Monee, IL
01 September 2022

11983620R00056